Sibylle Delacroix

Grains of Sand

Owlkids Books

Published in North America in 2018 by Owlkids Books Inc.

Published in France under the title *Graines de sable* in 2017 by Bayard Éditions.

Owlkids Books acknowledges the financial support of the Canada Council for the Arts, the Ontario Arts Council, the Government of Canada through the Canada Book Fund (CBF), and the Government of Ontario through the Ontario Media Development Corporation's Book Initiative for our publishing activities.

Published in Canada by
Owlkids Books Inc.
10 Lower Spadina Avenue
Toronto, ON M5V 2Z2

Published in the United States by
Owlkids Books Inc.
1700 Fourth Street
Berkeley, CA 94710

Library and Archives Canada Cataloguing in Publication

Delacroix, Sibylle [Graines de sable. English]   Grains of sand / [written and illustrated by]
Sibylle Delacroix ; translated by Karen Li.

Translation of: Graines de sable. ISBN 978-1-77147-205-0 (hardcover)

    I. Li, Karen, translator II. Title. III.Title: Graines de sable. English

PZ7.D45Gra 2018   j843'.92   C2017-904440-0

Library of Congress Control Number: 2017946103

Manufactured in Dongguan, China, in October 2017, by Toppan Leefung Packaging & Printing (Dongguan) Co., Ltd.
Job #BAYDC52

A   B   C   D   E   F

Publisher of Chirp, chickaDEE and OWL | Owlkids Books is a division of   Bayard
www.owlkidsbooks.com   CANADA

Today was the last day of our vacation.

When we get home, Ulysses still has water
in his eyes. I am as blue as the sea.

And my shoes are filled with sand.

"What are you doing?"
asks Ulysses.

"I have all these grains of sand, and I don't
want to throw them away… I know! Let's plant them!"

"Oh! What do you think will grow?"

"Let's see..."

"Maybe a field of beach umbrellas to wave hello to the sun?"

"Or a forest of pinwheels

to fill the sails of a boat."

"How about a crop of ice cream? Lemon-flavored, please!"

"Perhaps a castle strong enough
to stand against the tide."

"I'd give it a good soaking with a giant wave of laughter."

"Maybe our grains will grow into a beach...
powdered gold to sift through our fingers."

"Or to fill the sandman's bags..." says Daddy,
who sees me rubbing my eyes.

Before I drift off, I hear Daddy promise that we'll go back to the beach next year and harvest new grains of sand.